Read-to-Me Treasury Classics

Bedtime

Disney PRESS
New York

All books illustrated by the storybook artists at Disney Publishing Worldwide.

Copyright © 2011 Disney Enterprises, Inc. All rights reserved. Published by Disney Press, an imprint
of Disney Book Group. No part of this book may be reproduced or transmitted in any form or by any means,
electronic or mechanical, including photocopying, recording, or by any information storage and retrieval system,
without written permission from the publisher.
For information address Disney Press, 114 Fifth Avenue, New York, New York 10011-5690.

Printed in the United Sates of America

First Edition

3 5 7 9 10 8 6 4 2

G942-9090-6-13287

ISBN 978-1-4231-2394-1

For more Disney Press fun, visit www.disneybooks.com

SUSTAINABLE FORESTRY INITIATIVE
Certified Sourcing
www.sfiprogram.org
SFI-00993
This Label Applies to Text Stock Only

CONTENTS

Introduction ❧ 4

Peter Pan ❧ 7

The Jungle Book ❧ 73

The Aristocats ❧ 139

Toy Story ❧ 205

The Tigger Movie ❧ 271

Monsters, Inc. ❧ 337

❧ INTRODUCTION ❧

*Help Sulley and Mike return Boo safely to her room; bounce along with
Tigger as he searches for his long-lost family; soar over Never Land with
Peter Pan. . . . You and your child can share these magical adventures
and more in this treasury of beloved Disney bedtime tales.*

Dear Parents and Caregivers:

Educators will tell you that reading aloud for at least fifteen minutes a day is
one of the best gifts you can give your child. Not only will you help your child
develop language skills but you will be setting the foundation for a love of books
and a desire to read. You will also be spending time with your loved one. What
could be better than that?

The Whens and Whys of Reading Aloud

You can read aloud to your child whenever you have the time or whenever your
child hands you a book and says, "Please read to me." Bedtime and naptime
make a nice routine time for reading. But don't forget to take along a book when
you visit the pediatrician or dentist. Reading can be a comforting diversion. For
trips on a plane, bus, or train, reading can help pass the time.

Depending on the age of your child, he or she might want to sit with
this treasury and flip through the pages, talk aloud to the characters, or raise
questions about what happens on a particular page. Be around to answer or
comment. The more you and your child become involved with the story, the
more an appreciation for books, language, and storytelling will grow.

You might ask your child to choose one of his or her favorite stories. Don't be
surprised if after being introduced to a new tale, your child asks you to read it over
and over again. Revisiting stories helps young children make connections between
the stories they hear and the pictures and words they see. They begin to be able
to predict what is going to happen next. Familiarity makes your child feel like an
expert—a positive feeling that is then attached
to the whole reading experience. Repetition
not only helps children develop a comfort
zone with books but it also reinforces
important letter- and word-recognition skills.

If your child shows an interest in words, you might pause at certain places in the text and ask questions such as: can you find the word *Roquefort*? Can you find the names of Andy's toys? Associating written words with storytelling is an important reading-readiness skill. But remember to let your child set the pace and tell you what he or she wants to learn or talk about.

Quick Tips

Here are some hints to help you and your little reader on your way:

- Set a reading mood. Let your little listener settle in and, perhaps by looking at the cover, start thinking about the story.
- Children have different attention spans. Note that each of the stories in this treasury is divided into sections, so you have a natural place to stop, then start again at another sitting.
- Put lots of expression into your reading—if possible, change your voice to fit each character.
- Keep your child involved. Invite him or her to turn the pages when it's time.
- At the end of each section, you might raise questions such as: what do you think will happen to Boo? Will her new monster friends help her to safety? Do you think Mowgli will ever leave the jungle? Never pry an interpretation out of your child. Let your child's interests be your guide.
- Don't rush. A slow-paced read gives your child time to explore the pictures and make his or her own mental map of what's happening in the story. Plus, it reinforces the message that you enjoy spending quiet time together.

So now it's time to find that cozy nook, to cuddle and snuggle with your child, and to share a Disney read-to-me story together. You're ready to embark on the magical road to reading!

The Editors

The Lost Shadow

Long ago in London, there lived three children—
Wendy, John, and Michael Darling. Each night, Wendy
told her brothers stories before bed. John and Michael
loved all of Wendy's stories. But their favorites were
about Peter Pan, a boy who lived in a faraway place
called Never Land and refused to grow up.

On this particular night, Mr. Darling was quite angry.
His sons were pretending to be pirates, and Michael had
drawn a treasure map on his father's last clean shirt. Mr.
Darling blamed Wendy for filling the boys' heads with
stories of Peter Pan.

"This is your last night in the nursery, young lady,"
Mr. Darling said. "It is time for you to grow up."

Mrs. Darling tucked the children into bed, and before long, they were fast asleep.

Suddenly two figures appeared outside the house. It was Peter Pan and his fairy friend, Tinker Bell!

The Darlings' nursery was a familiar place to Peter. He liked to sit in the shadows and listen to Wendy's stories about Never Land. But on his last visit, Peter had lost his shadow. Tonight he had come to get it back.

"Well done, Tink, you've found it," Peter whispered when Tinker Bell discovered his shadow in a drawer.

But the shadow was in no hurry to be
caught. It flitted and skittered around
the room! Peter charged after it, making
such a racket that Wendy woke up.

Finally Peter caught his shadow. He tried to reattach it, but it just wouldn't stick! Wendy offered to sew it on.

"Oh, Peter, I knew you would come!" she said as she sewed. "Tonight's my last night in the nursery. I have to grow up tomorrow!"

"But that means no more stories!" cried Peter. "I won't have it! Come on. We're going to Never Land. You'll never grow up there!"

Wendy hurriedly woke her brothers. Peter Pan sprinkled some of Tinker Bell's pixie dust over the children and told them to think happy thoughts.

"We're flying!" shouted Wendy, John, and Michael as they followed Peter and Tink out of the nursery window. They soared over the rooftops of London. Peter laughed with glee as he pointed up into the sky.

"There it is, Wendy. Never Land . . . second star to the right and straight on till morning."

The Wendy Bird

Finally Never Land appeared.

"Look, John," cried Wendy. "Mermaid Lagoon!"

"And the Indian Camp!" yelled John.

"There's the pirate ship and its crew," added Michael.

"It's just like in your stories, Wendy!"

On the ship below, a pirate named Captain Hook was busy scheming with his first mate, Mr. Smee. Peter had chopped off Hook's hand in a sword fight and fed it to a crocodile. The crocodile thought it was delicious, and now he followed the pirate everywhere, hoping for another bite. Hook wanted revenge!

Suddenly Captain Hook looked up and saw Peter flying in the clouds. He quickly shot a cannonball at Peter and the children. Luckily, it zoomed by and they didn't get hurt.

"Quick, Tink! Take Wendy and the boys to the island," yelled Peter. While Peter distracted Hook, Tinker Bell hurried toward the island. She flew so fast that Wendy, John, and Michael fell far behind. The fairy thought Peter Pan was spending too much time with Wendy. She was jealous, and she had a plan.

Tinker Bell went to see the Lost Boys. She told the
boys that Peter wanted them to shoot the Wendy bird
out of the sky.

The Lost Boys grabbed their slingshots. "Ready . . .
aim . . . fire!" they shouted.

Rocks flew everywhere. They hit Wendy and sent her
tumbling from the sky!

Fortunately, Peter arrived in time to save her. But he was very angry with Tink. He banished her for a whole week!

Tiger Lily

While John and Michael played with the Lost Boys, Peter took Wendy to visit the mermaids in the lagoon.

Suddenly Peter spotted Captain Hook and Smee. They had kidnapped Tiger Lily, the Indian chief's daughter, and tied her to a rock.

Peter revealed himself and challenged Hook to a duel. As they fought, the tide got closer and closer to Tiger Lily's head. Finally, Peter backed Captain Hook into the water, where the crocodile snapped, waiting for another taste! Hook shouted and swam away as quickly as possible.

Peter swooped down and rescued Tiger Lily. He brought her safely back to her village, where there was a great celebration in his honor.

The only person who didn't celebrate was Tinker Bell, who was very angry at being banished.

Tinker Bell Betrays Peter

Tinker Bell was so upset that she didn't even notice Smee sneak up behind her. He shoved her in his cap and brought her to Captain Hook.

"We sail in the morning," Hook told Tinker Bell. He promised to take Wendy with him if Tink would tell him where Peter's hideout was.

With Tinker Bell's help, Captain Hook found his way to Peter's hideout. The pirates surrounded the tree and waited for the Lost Boys to come out.

Meanwhile, inside Peter's hideout, all was cozy and quiet. Wendy tucked the boys into bed and sang a song about the wonders of a real mother. By the time Wendy finished singing, John and Michael were so homesick that they wanted to leave for London at once. Even the Lost Boys wanted to go.

But Peter did not want to leave Never Land. "Go back and grow up!" he said stubbornly. "I'm warnin' you, once you're grown up, you can never come back!"

One by one, the boys walked
out of Peter's hideout . . . right
into the arms of the waiting pirates!

"Now to take care of Master Peter Pan!" Hook chuckled as he lowered a beautifully wrapped package into the hideout.

Inside, Peter Pan picked up the package. He was just untying the bow when Tinker Bell appeared. She flew at the box, pulling it as far from Peter as she could. Suddenly the gift began to smoke. And then . . . *kaboom!*

Peter Pan to the Rescue

Back on the pirate ship, Wendy refused to join Captain Hook. "Join me or walk the plank!" he cried.

So, with tears trickling down her cheeks, Wendy walked the plank. One step, then another, closer and closer to the edge, until finally. . . she jumped!

But there was no splash! Peter had saved
Wendy just in the nick of time.
"This time you've gone too far!" Peter shouted.

As Hook and Peter began to duel, John, Michael, and the Lost Boys climbed to the crow's nest. The Lost Boys threw rocks at the pirates. John even hit them on the head with his umbrella. One by one, the pirates were defeated. All except Hook, who was still fighting Peter.

Peter and Hook battled it out on the ship's yardarm, which had swung over the water. Peter grabbed Hook's sword, but then decided to let him go. But the pirate had been humiliated. He took a swipe at Peter, lost his balance, and plunged into the water . . .

. . . right into the jaws of the crocodile.

Peter took control of Hook's ship. Wendy and the rest of the children cheered, "Hooray for Captain Pan!"

"Could you tell me, sir, where we're sailing?" asked Wendy with a smile.

"To London, madam," Peter replied.

Tinker Bell sprinkled the ship with pixie dust, and soon it rose into the air. Below it, Never Land grew smaller and smaller, until finally it disappeared.

As they approached London, Wendy and her brothers said good-bye to Peter and the Lost Boys. They knew they would never forget this adventure!

At home, Wendy's mother shook her awake. She had fallen asleep by the window.

As Wendy and her parents peered out at the sky, a ship sailed across the moon.

"You know," Mr. Darling said, his arm around his daughter, "I have the strangest feeling I've seen that ship before . . . a long time ago."

And indeed he had.

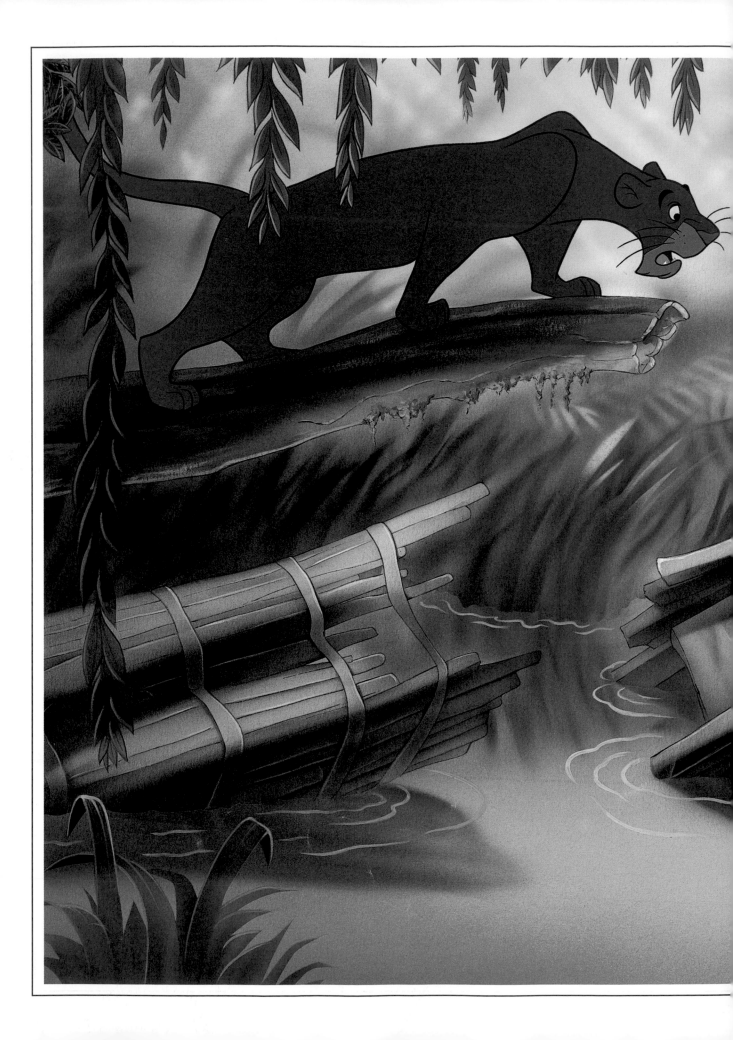

The Man-Cub

Bagheera the panther was walking
through the jungle one day when he heard
a strange cry. He walked to the river and
found a man-cub floating in a broken boat.

Bagheera looked at the man-cub. The nearest man-village was far away, and the cub needed a mother. Finally he brought the boy to a wolf family's lair.

"We will call him Mowgli and raise him as our own," the wolves said.

And so it was that Mowgli came to be raised in the jungle.

Over time, Mowgli grew into a boy. The wolves could no longer protect him from the dangers of the jungle. Shere Khan the tiger was one of these dangers. He hated humans and wanted nothing more than to get rid of Mowgli!

One night the wolves held a council. "Life in the jungle is dangerous for humans," they told Bagheera. "You must take Mowgli back to the man-village."

In the Jungle

The next day, Bagheera and Mowgli left to take a walk in the jungle. As it grew darker, Mowgli started to feel sleepy. He wanted to turn back, but Bagheera explained that he couldn't return to the jungle. They were going to the nearest man-village instead.

As night fell, Bagheera started to fall asleep. Suddenly, Kaa the snake appeared. Kaa's tail coiled around Mowgli. When Bagheera saw what was happening, he hit Kaa on the head. Kaa slithered away, grumbling to himself.

The next day, Bagheera and Mowgli woke up to an earthquake. The ground shook as a patrol of elephants, led by Colonel Hathi, marched by.

Mowgli got down on all fours and joined the parade.

"I'll have no man-cub in my jungle," declared Colonel Hathi.

"The man-cub is with me," interrupted Bagheera. "I'm taking him to the man-village."

Bagheera wanted to bring Mowgli to the man-village right away, before anything else could happen to him. But Mowgli refused. He held on tightly to a small tree. Finally Bagheera gave up.

"From now on, you're on your own!" he shouted as he walked off.

Mowgli sat down with his head hung low until he heard sounds coming from a nearby bush. It was Baloo the bear.

Baloo saw that Mowgli needed
some lessons on how to survive
in the jungle. He taught the
man-cub everything he knew,
like how to find delicacies such
as ants, bananas, and coconuts.

The new friends spent the next few days doing what Baloo liked best: nothing but eating and relaxing!

They didn't know that Bagheera was always close by, making sure no harm came to them.

King Louie

One day, Mowgli ran into a group of monkeys. They grabbed him by the arms and began to swing through the treetops.

Baloo shouted at the monkeys, but he could not stop them from taking Mowgli.

Bagheera heard the shouting
and came running. He and Baloo
had to save their man-cub!

The monkeys took
Mowgli to meet their
leader, King Louie. He
wanted Mowgli to teach
him how to make fire!

Up above, Baloo and Bagheera watched the monkeys. They had to find a way into their temple.

Just then Baloo had an idea.

Baloo disguised himself as a monkey and entered the temple, dancing and singing. King Louie took Baloo by the hand and crossed the temple's courtyard, swinging to the jungle beat.

While Baloo distracted King Louie, Bagheera tried to rescue Mowgli. But every time he got close to the man-cub, Mowgli moved farther and farther away.

Suddenly, Baloo's costume fell off. "It's Baloo the bear!" screamed a monkey.

At that moment, King Louie's temple started to crumble. Baloo asked King Louie to help him hold up the temple's roof. As soon as King Louie was in place, Baloo let go of his end and ran away into the jungle with Mowgli and Bagheera.

That night, Bagheera persuaded
Baloo that Mowgli was in danger
in the jungle. But when Baloo
tried to convince Mowgli that he
belonged in the man-village,
Mowgli ran away.

Shere Khan

The next evening, Shere Khan overheard Bagheera say that Mowgli had run off. If the boy was alone, this was Shere Khan's chance to catch him!

Mowgli, meanwhile, had run into Kaa. Kaa wrapped the man-cub in his coils and began to squeeze.

Suddenly Kaa felt a tug on his tail. It was Shere Khan!

Shere Khan flexed his talons. He wanted Kaa to give him the man-cub.

Kaa had no choice but to agree. There was just one problem. While he had been talking to Shere Khan, Mowgli had gotten away!

Mowgli ran through the jungle until he came upon a flock of vultures. The vultures thought the man-cub was a strange-looking bird and decided to keep him company.

Just then there was a terrible roar! Shere Khan pounced!

Mowgli turned to face the tiger, who suddenly fell backward! Baloo had arrived and was holding on to Shere Khan's tail.

The vultures picked up Mowgli and flew him to safety.

Suddenly, the sky darkened and lightning struck, setting fire to a nearby tree. Mowgli quickly grabbed a blazing branch and stormed toward Shere Khan.

Mowgli tied the burning
branch to Shere Khan's tail.
The tiger gave a cry of pain
and ran away.

As the vultures flew down to congratulate the man-cub, they found Mowgli kneeling beside his dear friend Baloo. Shere Khan had hit him hard, and he was not moving.

After a long pause, Baloo opened his
eyes. He sat up and acted like nothing
had happened.

The Man-Village

Shere Khan had been scared away, but he had not been defeated. Sadly, Mowgli realized that his friends were right. It was time for him to return to the man-village.

As they neared the village, Mowgli noticed a pretty girl fetching water from the river's edge.

Baloo and Bagheera watched as Mowgli ran to help the girl carry the pot full of water. As Mowgli followed her into the man-village, he turned around to give his animal friends one last smile.

Baloo and Bagheera were sad to see their little
friend go, but they were happy that he'd found a
place where he belonged. And so the friends
sang a merry song as they returned to the jungle
once more, arm in arm.

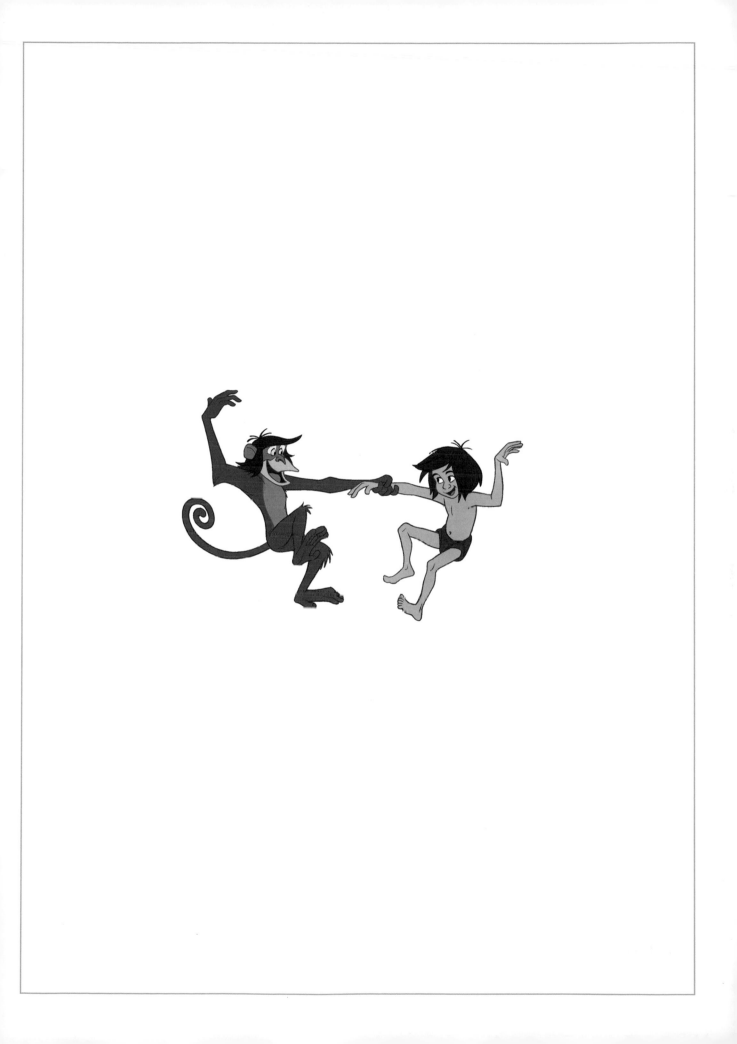

Madame's News

Long ago, in the city of Paris, there lived a very grand lady named Madame Adelaide Bonfamille.

Duchess, a charming white Angora, and her three kittens—Berlioz, Toulouse, and Marie—were all very happy to be part of Madame's family. So was Edgar, the butler.

Madame and her cats lived in a style that was truly aristocratic. In fact, Duchess and her kittens were Aristocats!

"Oh, Edgar, I'm expecting my lawyer, Georges Hautecourt," Madame said as she entered her beautiful home.

As she waited, Madame watched each of the kittens display a different talent. Marie sang, Toulouse painted, and Berlioz played the piano.

Suddenly the door opened and Georges walked into the room.

"I've asked you here on an important legal matter," said Madame.

As Duchess and the kittens gathered around, Madame told Georges that she wanted to leave her entire fortune to her precious Aristocats.

Meanwhile, through the pipes in his room, Edgar listened in on Madame's conversation. The butler was shocked to learn that he would not inherit anything from Madame until all the cats had died.

Edgar had always been jealous of Duchess and her kittens. Now he had even more reason to hate them.

"Those cats have got to go!" he hissed.

The Plan

Edgar soon cooked up a nasty scheme to get rid of Duchess and her kittens. He planned to lull the cats to sleep, drive them into the countryside, and leave them behind. He poured an entire bottle of sleeping pills into a pot of warm milk. Edgar knew the Aristocats would never suspect a thing.

Duchess and the kittens lapped up the creamy liquid. Berlioz even invited Roquefort the mouse to dunk his big cracker into the milk.

Everyone ate until they were full. Then Roquefort staggered back to his hole and fell fast asleep. Duchess and the kittens were also feeling tired. The sleeping pills had worked!

Soon Duchess and her kittens had fallen into a
deep, deep sleep. As the moon rose in the night sky,
Edgar crept in and gathered up the cats.

Edgar placed the basket in the sidecar of his motorcycle and headed for the country. He was far from Madame's house when he ran into a bloodhound and a basset hound who came from a farm near the road.

The dogs chased Edgar into a river. The basket holding the sleeping Aristocats tumbled off the sidecar and came to rest in the soft grass under a bridge.

Duchess and her kittens awoke to a
thunderstorm. They did not know where
they were or how they had gotten there.
Duchess gathered Marie, Toulouse, and
Berlioz to her. "It will be all right, darlings,"
she said softly. But even she was frightened.

Back at home, the storm awakened Madame. Knowing her cats were afraid of thunder, she went to check on them.

Madame gently pulled back the drapes over their little bed. "They're gone!" she screamed. She looked everywhere. She even asked Edgar if he knew where they were, but the butler said nothing.

O'Malley

The next morning, as the sun warmed the countryside, Duchess heard a happy voice floating down the river. It was Abraham DeLacy Giuseppe Casey Thomas O'Malley, the alley cat. His friends called him O'Malley for short.

O'Malley was taken with Duchess the minute he spotted her across the river.

"Why . . . your eyes are like sapphires," he cooed to Duchess.

But Duchess interrupted the handsome tomcat. "We are in a great deal of trouble, Monsieur O'Malley!" she told him. She explained what had happened, and O'Malley offered to help them get back to the city.

O'Malley snuck the Aristocats onto a milk van. "All aboard!" he called out.

As the van started up, Duchess thanked the alley cat for all he had done. Suddenly, the van hit some big rocks in the road.

"Marie!" screamed Duchess. O'Malley turned just in time to see Marie fall out of the van.

O'Malley grabbed Marie and scrambled to catch up with the van.

"Thank you for saving my life, Mr. O'Malley," Marie said meekly. It was then that O'Malley decided he'd better go back to Paris with the Aristocats.

A Close Call

The next morning, Duchess, O'Malley, and the kittens woke up hungry. They helped themselves to breakfast from a can of milk.

Just as they began to eat, the deliveryman spotted them in his rearview mirror. He slammed on his brakes and angrily chased the cats out of his van.

O'Malley and the Aristocats started walking across
a large wooden bridge. Suddenly they felt the ground
rumble, and a train appeared. It was bearing down on
the cats at a frightening speed.

"Quick! Duck beneath the bridge," O'Malley called.

The bridge shook violently as the train
roared over it. O'Malley and Duchess held
on to the kittens as tightly as they could,
but little Marie slipped.

"Mama!" she cried, falling down to the rushing river below.

O'Malley dived into the river. Duchess dashed to the end of a log and scooped Marie up just as O'Malley lifted her out of the water.

But O'Malley wasn't the best swimmer, and he was carried farther and farther downriver. Fortunately, the river flowed into calmer waters, and O'Malley floated right into the path of two white geese. Duchess and the kittens were relieved when the kindhearted geese carried O'Malley safely to shore.

By nighttime, the cats had reached the city. Duchess was anxious to reach Madame's house, but the kittens were so tired that O'Malley convinced Duchess to spend the night at his nearby penthouse.

When they arrived at O'Malley's place, they found that some of his musician friends had dropped by for a jam session.

O'Malley was worried that Duchess would not like the jazz music his friends played. But Duchess was quick to react to the bouncy tune. "Your music is so different . . . and exciting!" she called out.

Toulouse, Berlioz, and Marie joined in the fun, too. Now the band was really jamming.

After the band left, Duchess and O'Malley took a quiet moment for themselves.

"Your eyes really are like sapphires," he said to her warmly.

The kittens listened as O'Malley proposed to Duchess. But Duchess couldn't accept. Madame still needed her. She and the kittens had to return home.

Home at Last

The next morning, O'Malley, Duchess, and the kittens arrived on Madame's street. Roquefort watched from the window as O'Malley and Duchess sadly said their good-byes.

Unfortunately, Edgar had seen the cats, too. The nasty butler threw a big sack over them. Duchess and the kittens meowed for help as loudly as they could.

Up in her room, Madame heard the cats' cries for help. Thinking Duchess and the kittens had returned, she rushed to the front door. But there were no cats in sight. Edgar had hidden the Aristocats in the kitchen.

Roquefort ran to see if Duchess and the kittens were all right.

"Go get O'Malley, Roquefort! Quick!" Duchess cried.

The little mouse soon caught up with O'Malley. He told the cat what had happened, and O'Malley asked Roquefort to track down his gang of alley cats. "Just tell them O'Malley sent you!"

O'Malley to the Rescue

Roquefort was afraid that the alley cats might eat him. He *was* a mouse, after all! But when he mentioned O'Malley's name, the alley cats quickly agreed to help.

At Madame's house, O'Malley saw Edgar carry a sack into the stables. The Aristocats were in the sack!

O'Malley watched Edgar lock the cats in a big trunk. He was going to ship them all the way to Timbuktu, Africa!

There was no time to lose. O'Malley leaped onto Edgar's back, scratching and clawing the evil butler.

O'Malley's gang arrived in the nick of time and managed to overpower the butler. While the alley cats were keeping Edgar busy, Roquefort picked the lock on the trunk. When he got the lock open, O'Malley lifted the lid and let Duchess and the kittens out of the sack.

With one swift kick from Frou Frou the horse, the butler ended up inside the big trunk. The alley cats pushed the trunk out onto the street just as the baggage van pulled up to the stables.

"Well, this must be the trunk that's going to Timbuktu," the driver said. He picked up the heavy trunk and put it in the back of the van.

Madame Bonfamille was happy beyond words to be reunited with her beloved Aristocats. Realizing that Duchess and O'Malley were in love, she immediately invited him to live with them.

"Now, my pets, a little closer together!" she cried, and took a portrait of her happy little family.

The Birthday Party

Andy had a big imagination. He loved playing with all his toys, but his all-time favorite was Sheriff Woody. The two had been the best of friends ever since Andy was in kindergarten. They had fought bad guys, rescued good guys, and had all kinds of exciting adventures together. Andy took Woody everywhere.

"Okay, birthday boy. Go get your sister. It's almost time for your party," Andy's mom called from downstairs.

Andy dropped Woody on the bed and scooped up his little sister, Molly. "See you later, Woody," he called as he left his room.

Woody sat up and rubbed his head. "Okay, everybody, coast is clear!" he shouted.

One by one, Andy's toys stood up and started to talk. But Woody didn't have time for howdy-dos. He had big news.

Andy's family was moving in a week, and Woody wanted to make sure that none of the toys got lost.

But that wasn't their only worry. Today was Andy's birthday. And birthdays meant new toys. Someone might get replaced!

The toys watched nervously as Andy's friends walked up the front steps.

"Take a look at all those presents!" Hamm exclaimed.

"They're getting bigger!" Rex cried out. Each present seemed bigger and more worrisome than the last.

Woody sent the Green Army Men downstairs to spy on Andy's party.

The soldiers set up a baby monitor inside a potted plant. As each present was unwrapped, they sent the news back to Andy's room.

Luckily, nothing sounded too threatening.

Then, just when the toys thought they were safe, Andy's mom found one last present.

Andy and his friends burst into the bedroom. They ran around happily, then rushed out again—leaving the mystery toy on the bed.

In the excitement, Woody fell on the floor. The other toys watched anxiously as he climbed back up onto the bed.

The new toy turned and blinked. "I am Buzz Lightyear, Space Ranger," he declared. Buzz thought he was a real space ranger. He didn't know he was a toy!

With Buzz in Andy's room, everything changed. The cowboy posters on the wall were replaced with space posters. Andy stopped wearing his cowboy hat and started running through the house in a space costume. Even the other toys seemed to prefer Buzz.

But the biggest
change was at bedtime.
When Andy climbed
under the covers, he
took Buzz with him
instead of Woody!

Pizza Planet

One night, Andy's mom suggested a trip to Pizza Planet. She told Andy that he could only take one toy with him.

Woody wanted to make sure he was chosen. He made a plan to knock Buzz behind the desk, where Andy couldn't find him. But instead, Buzz fell out the window.

Andy searched high and low for Buzz, but he couldn't find the space ranger anywhere. Finally he grabbed Woody. Then he ran downstairs and hopped into the car. As the car's motor started up, a small figure emerged from the bushes and leaped onto the car's bumper. It was Buzz!

When Andy's mom stopped at a gas station, Buzz jumped into the backseat with Woody.

But Buzz wasn't pleased to see Woody. The space ranger leaped onto the cowboy, and they began to fight. The two toys tumbled out of the car and landed on the pavement.

Suddenly, Andy's mom drove off—without them! Woody and Buzz were stranded at the gas station.

Luckily, Woody spotted a Pizza Planet delivery truck. The truck could take the toys to Andy!

At Pizza Planet, Woody quickly spotted Andy. With a little luck, he and Buzz could jump into Molly's stroller.

"Okay, Buzz, get ready and . . . Buzz?" Woody turned around to see Buzz striding toward the Rocket Ship Crane Game. The space ranger thought it was a real spaceship.

Buzz climbed into the Rocket Ship Crane Game, and Woody followed. He was still hoping he could make Buzz return to Andy.

Suddenly, the machine started whirring. Then the claw dropped—right on Buzz. Woody grabbed Buzz's feet and tried to drag him back down. But it was no use.

"All right! Double prizes!" shouted the winner, seeing the two toys.

To Woody's horror, he saw that the boy was Sid, Andy's nasty neighbor.

All the toys in Andy's room knew Sid. He was the meanest kid on the block. From Andy's bedroom window, Woody had seen Sid torture many toys.

Sid looked at Buzz and Woody with evil glee. "Let's go home and . . . play!" he said with a wicked laugh.

Woody knew they were doomed.

Sid's bedroom was dark and eerie. He had lots of scary tools that he used for toy "operations."

Suddenly, Woody and Buzz heard strange rustling sounds. Broken toys crept out of the darkness. Sid had turned his once-normal toys into terrifying mutants!

Woody grabbed Buzz, trying to protect himself and the space ranger from the mutant toys.

Buzz and Woody ran into the hall—and straight into Scud, Sid's vicious dog! Panicked, the two toys fled.

Buzz ducked through an open door. Suddenly, he heard: "Calling Buzz Lightyear! This is Star Command!" The voice continued, "The world's greatest superhero, now the world's greatest toy!"

It was a TV commercial for Buzz Lightyear *toys*!

Buzz was stunned. He walked to the stairs. He knew he could fly . . . couldn't he? Gathering all his courage, Buzz climbed to the top of the stair railing—and leaped.

"To infinity and beyond!" he cried.

For a moment, Buzz seemed to hang in the air. Then—*CRASH!* Buzz fell onto the stair landing, and his left arm broke off.

Finally Buzz understood the truth: he wasn't a space ranger. He was a toy.

Upstairs, Woody searched for Buzz. He peeked into a bedroom and saw Sid's little sister, Hannah, playing with the space ranger. She had found him and added him to her tea party.

Woody waited until Hannah left the room, then ran to help Buzz. But Buzz didn't want help. "Look at me," he moaned. "I can't even fly out the window."

Suddenly Woody had an idea!

Woody ran to Sid's bedroom window and called out to Andy's toys.

The cowboy threw them a string of Christmas lights—an escape line from Sid's bedroom. But the toys in Andy's room remembered that Woody had made Buzz fall out the window. They refused to help him.

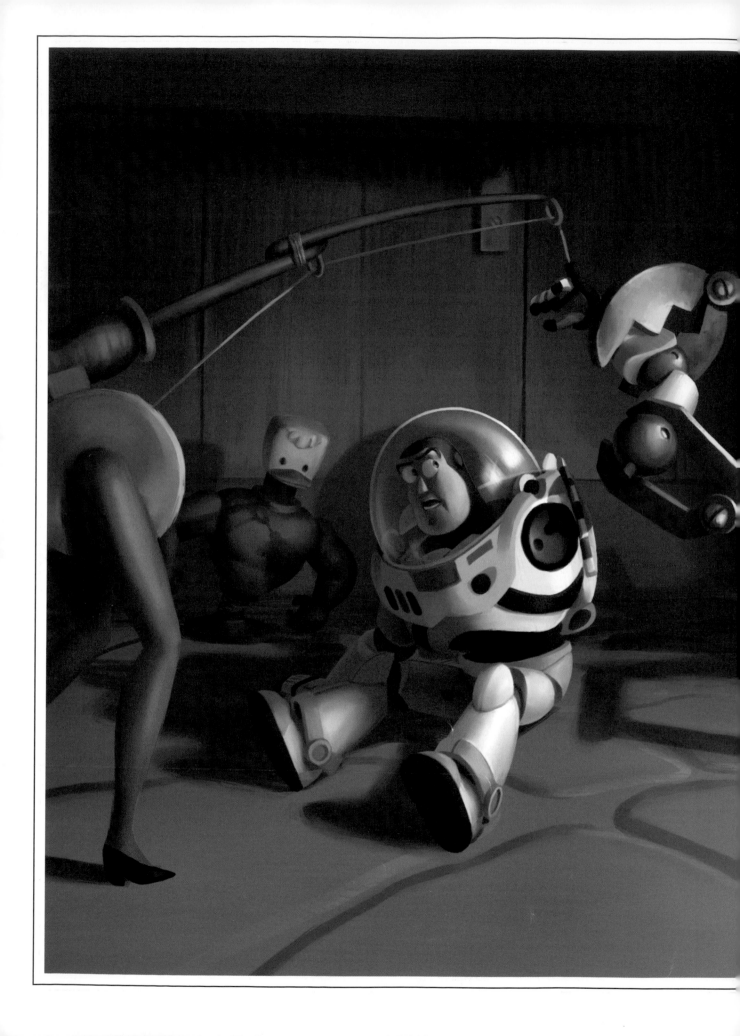

Woody felt terrible. When he turned back into Sid's room, he saw that the mutant toys had surrounded Buzz! Woody tried to fight them off, but they grabbed Buzz's arm and pushed Woody away.

After a moment, the mutants stepped away from the space ranger. Buzz sat up in surprise, flexing his left arm. Sid's mutant toys had fixed him! Even though they looked scary, the mutant toys were friendly.

Blastoff!

Just then, Sid burst into the room. He stuck Woody under a crate and strapped a rocket onto Buzz's back. Blastoff was scheduled for the next morning.

All night, Woody pleaded with Buzz to return to Andy. "Over in that house is a kid who thinks you are the greatest. And it's not because you're a space ranger. It's because you're a toy. You are *his* toy," Woody said.

Finally Buzz realized that Woody was right. Being a toy was important.

The space ranger knew it was time to get back to Andy! He ran over to Woody and freed him from the crate.

Suddenly, the alarm clock rang. Sid jumped out of bed. "Time for liftoff!" he yelled, grabbing Buzz and running outside.

Woody knew he had to do something fast. He gathered the mutant toys and laid out a rescue plan. "We'll have to break a few rules," he told the mutants. "But if it works, it'll help everyone."

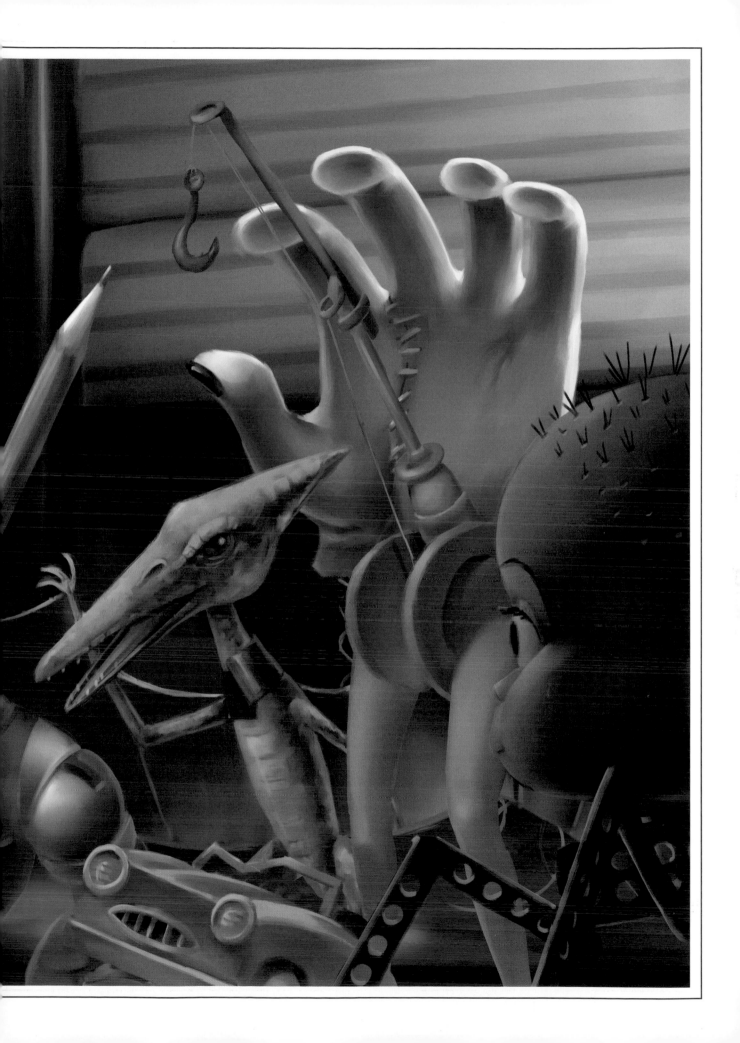

While some of the mutants distracted Scud and Hannah, Woody and the others jumped onto a skateboard and raced down the stairs, shooting out into the backyard.

Outside, Sid was preparing to launch Buzz into outer space. With a cruel grin, he leaned over to light the big rocket's fuse.

"Ten, nine, eight, seven . . ." he counted.

Suddenly Sid heard someone say, "Reach for the sky!" It was Woody, lying nearby. Sid turned and stared.

One by one, the mutant toys stood up and staggered out of the sandbox, splashed out of a puddle, and crawled out from under the dog dish! Slowly and steadily, they surrounded the human boy.

"From now on, you must take good care of your toys.
Because if you don't, we'll find out," Woody warned Sid. He
leaned in very close and looked Sid right in the eye. "So
play nice!"

"AAAHH!" Sid threw up his arms and shrieked in terror.
Then he ran into the house and slammed the door.

Woody and Buzz couldn't stand around and cheer—the moving van was in front of Andy's house! If they didn't hurry, Andy would leave without them.

But Buzz couldn't fit through the fence. The rocket was still attached to his back!

By the time Woody helped Buzz through the fence, it was too late. Andy's car had driven off.

Woody and Buzz dashed after the moving van. Buzz grabbed a loose strap and climbed onto the rear of the van. He tried to help Woody up, too. But Scud had seen the two toys running, and he raced after them. The dog leaped up and grabbed Woody in his mouth, dragging him off the van.

"Nooooo!" Buzz yelled. He jumped onto Scud's head to save Woody.

Woody yanked open the back of the van and rummaged through the boxes until he found RC Car. Using the remote control, he sent RC back to pick up Buzz.

Andy's toys didn't understand what Woody was doing, and angrily threw him off the van! Luckily, Buzz and RC picked up Woody. Finally realizing what had happened, the other toys tried to help . . .

. . . but RC's batteries ran out. Woody watched, heartbroken, as the moving van chugged farther and farther away. Then Buzz realized—he still had the rocket on his back!

Woody lit the fuse.

As the rocket began to burn, RC picked up speed. Buzz and Woody hung on tight. The little car was moving so fast, they began to lift off the ground!

As they rose upward, Woody let go of RC, who landed in the van. Buzz and Woody whooshed into the sky.

Just as the rocket was about to explode, Buzz snapped open his space wings and broke free.

"Buzz, you're flying!" Woody exclaimed.

Buzz and Woody glided down toward Andy's car. While Andy was looking out the window, the two dropped through the car's open sunroof and landed safely on the backseat.

Hearing a thump, Andy looked over. "Woody! Buzz!" he shouted. He hugged them close, thrilled to have his two favorite toys back.

Woody and Buzz had made it home.

Everyone settled happily into the new house. All too soon, it was Christmas—which meant new toys.

"You aren't worried, are you?" Woody asked Buzz.

"No, no," Buzz replied nervously. "Are you?"

"Now, Buzz, what could Andy possibly get that is worse than you?" Woody teased.

The toys listened intently as Andy unwrapped his first present. Suddenly Buzz and Woody heard an unmistakable sound: *woof-woof!*

A puppy!

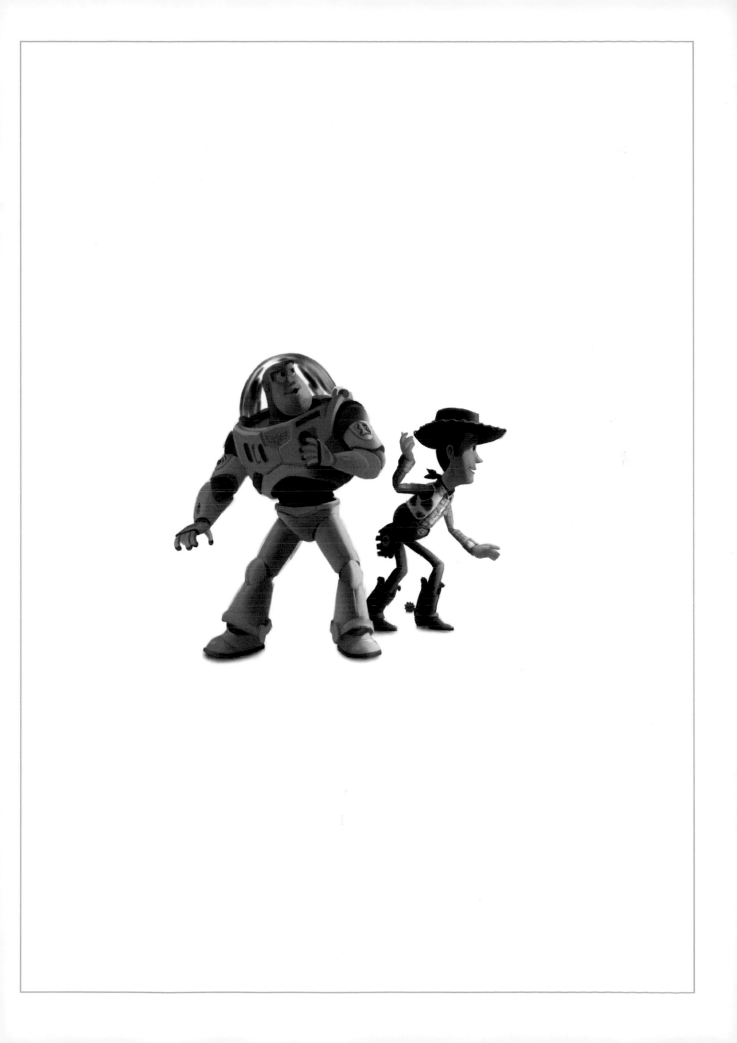

Tigger's Big Bounce

One blustery fall morning,
Tigger happily bounced through
the Hundred-Acre Wood.

Soon Tigger bounced right into Winnie the Pooh.
"Wanna go bouncin' with me?" asked Tigger.

"I *would* go bouncing with you," replied Pooh, "except
that I have to count my honeypots to make sure I have
enough for winter."

Next Tigger bounced into Piglet.
But Piglet could not bounce with Tigger,
either. He was busy collecting firewood. And
Kanga was busy sweeping.

So Tigger bounced all by himself until he BOUNCE-BOUNCE-BOUNCED onto a branch . . . which pushed over a great big rock . . . which rolled down a hill . . .

Boooooom!

. . . and landed right on Eeyore's house!
Eeyore's friends rushed over to see what
they might do to help.

Rabbit organized an enormous rock-moving machine. "Your attention, please," he said. "I have officially completed the plans." But the boulder wouldn't budge.

Finally, Tigger bounced up. He could see that a big bounce would get Rabbit's rock-moving machine going.

But Tigger's bounce made the machine get going too quickly!

"You ruin everything with your bouncing!" said Rabbit.

"But that's what tiggers do best," said Tigger.

"What we're trying to say," said Piglet, "is that we can't bounce like tiggers because . . ."

". . . we're not tiggers," finished Pooh sadly.

Roo followed Tigger as he walked off.
Suddenly Tigger brightened. "Say—if
there are other tiggers, we could all bounce
morning, noon, and nighty-night, too!"

The Family Tree

Tigger and Roo went to Owl to find out how to find other tiggers. Owl explained, "To find one's family, one must find one's family tree."

"Say, thanks for the tip, Beak-Lips!" Tigger cried as he and Roo bounced off.

Arriving with a great big bounce, Tigger asked his friends if they had seen any members of the tigger family tree. But no one had.

"I didn't know Tigger had a family," said Piglet.
"Seemed to be looking for 'em," added Eeyore.
"We must be supposed to help them," said Pooh.
"I often remember to forget these sorts of things."

After a long search, Tigger and Roo returned home without having found a single other tigger.

"If there were other tiggers, we could all bounce the Whoop-de-Dooper Loop-de-Looper Alley-Ooper Bounce," said Tigger sadly.

Wanting to be just like Tigger, Roo tried
the bounce, too. *Crash!* He landed in an open
closet—where he found a locket.

"It must have a picture of my tigger family
inside!" cried Tigger. But the locket was empty.

Meanwhile, Eeyore announced, "I found 'em—Tigger's family." He led Pooh and Piglet to a pond full of striped, bouncy frogs. Could this be Tigger's family?

"Tigger misses you very much," said Pooh to a frog. But the frog just hopped away.

Then, in a nearby tree, Pooh found some bees—*striped* bees. Bees that looked just a little bit like Tigger.

"Oh bother!" Pooh said when the bees started to chase him and Piglet and Eeyore. "I don't think these bees are the right sorts of tiggers."

Poor Tigger was no closer to finding his family.

"Why don't you write them a letter?" suggested Roo.

"Hoo-hoo-*hoo*!" hooted Tigger happily. And he began to write.

Tigger mailed his letter and waited for a response. But none came. Roo grew worried about his friend.

Kanga said, "As long as we care for him, he always will be one of our family."

A Letter for Tigger

The next day, Roo gathered everyone except Tigger at Owl's house. Roo wanted Owl to write a letter to Tigger from his family.

Owl began the letter: "Dear Tigger, Just a note to say . . ."

"Dress warmly," suggested Kanga.

"Eat well," added Pooh.

"Stay safe and sound," said Piglet.

"Keep smilin'," rumbled Eeyore.

"We're always there for you," said Roo.

Owl finished the letter: "Wishing you all the best,
Signed, Your Family."

The next morning, Tigger showed off the letter from his family. "They're comin' ta see me, TOMORROW!"

"Where does it say that?" asked Owl, surprised.

"Nowhere!" said Tigger. "'Cause with us tiggers ya gotta read betwixt the lines."

Now Roo had a new idea: the friends would pretend to be Tigger's long-lost family! They all painted on stripes and practiced their bouncing.

That evening, Tigger welcomed his family. "Let's all do what tiggers do best! That's bouncin', of course."

Roo tried to bounce the Whoop-de-Dooper Loop-de-Looper Alley-Ooper Bounce but crashed into the closet . . . again.

Roo's mask fell off. Then Tigger pulled off the others' masks as well.

Tigger was so disappointed. "There's a tigger family tree fulla my REAL family, and I'm gonna find 'em!" he said, and left.

Rabbit, Pooh, Piglet, Eeyore, and Roo
followed after Tigger. "Tigger! Tigger!"
they called into the raging snow.

Whoooooosssssshhh!

Deep in the forest, Tigger had just found a tree so grand and gleaming that it had to be the tigger family tree!

"Hoo-hoo-hoo!" called Tigger. But no one was home. Tigger sadly dropped his letter.

Tigger's letter soared off into the wind, and landed right in Roo's hand. He started running toward the giant tree, with the others right behind him.

"What are you guyses doing here?" Tigger asked.

"We came all this way to look for you!" explained Rabbit.

Tigger began to argue that he was waiting for his tigger family when a low rumble echoed through the valley.

Suddenly an avalanche was coming right at them!
Tigger bounced everyone to safety in his tree. But
the snow rolled Tigger toward a steep cliff!

Doing a perfect Whoop-de-Dooper
Loop-de-Looper Alley-Ooper Bounce,
Roo rescued Tigger.

Taking a long look at little Roo and
his other good friends, Tigger knew his
family had been with him all along.

The next day Tigger gave a party for all his friends.
As a special treat, he gave Roo his heart-shaped locket.
"Now wait half a minute!" Tigger cried excitedly.
"We need to take a family portrait to put in it."
And that's exactly what they did.

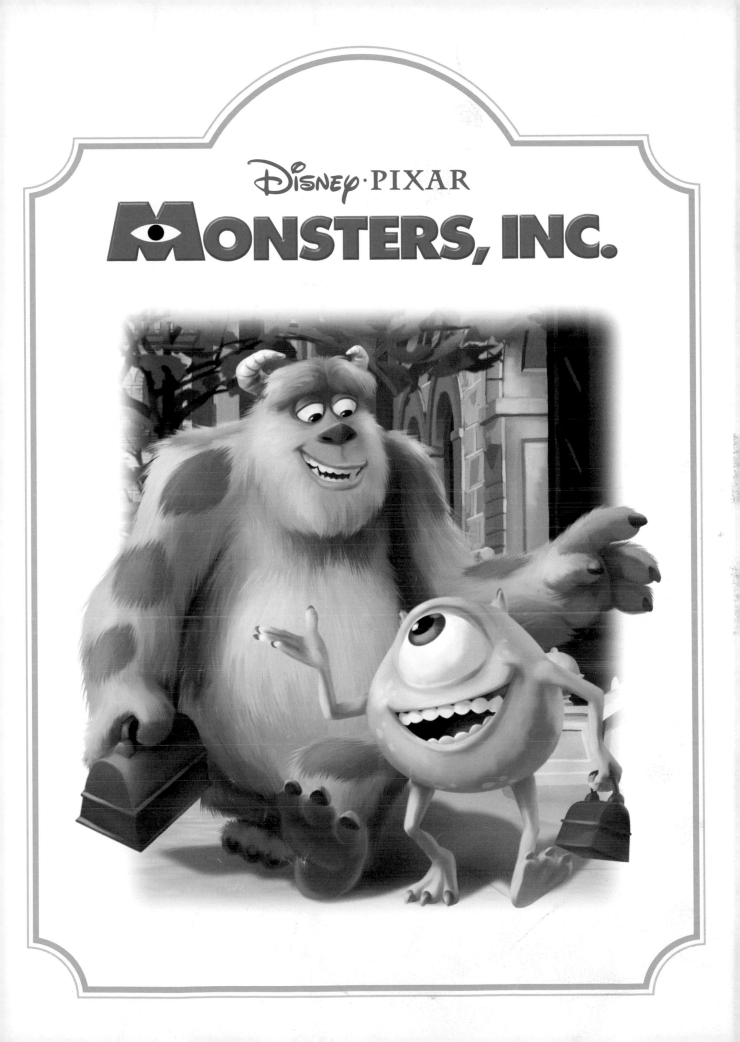

Screams and Scares

Late one night, a little boy awoke to see a monster in his bedroom. He screamed! Lights flashed and the room lit up. The little boy wasn't real. He was part of a training room at Monsters, Inc., where new employees learned to be Scarers.

The monster's teacher sighed and pointed to the closet door. "Leaving a door open is the worst mistake any employee can make, because . . ."

"It could let in a child!" shouted Mr. Waternoose, the CEO of Monsters, Inc.

The Scarers-in-Training gasped. They knew that children's screams powered Monstropolis. But letting a child into the world of monsters would be deadly to everyone!

Meanwhile, across town, James P. Sullivan was exercising. His assistant (and best friend), Mike Wazowski was coaching him.

Sulley was a professional Scarer, and he needed to keep in top shape.

"Feel the burn," Mike urged. "You call yourself a monster?!"

Sulley was famous for collecting more screams than
anyone else. That was important because the city was
having an energy shortage. Human kids were getting
harder to scare, and Monstropolis needed all the
screams it could get!

Sulley finished his exercises and he and Mike went
to work. It was time for another day of scaring!

In the locker room, a monster popped out at Mike. "Ahhh!" Mike shrieked.

It was Randall, another Scarer and Sulley's biggest rival. Randall was very jealous of Sulley. He would do anything to be the top Scarer.

Sulley led all the Scarers of Monsters, Inc.
onto the Scare Floor. Together, these were the
best scream collectors in the business.

The Scarers' assistants got to work, making their bosses as scary as possible. Finally they were ready to begin.

Doors dropped into each Scare station. Red lights flashed, and the Scarers walked through . . . right into the room of a sleeping child. Each Scarer hoped the child they were frightening would let out a good scream!

Suddenly, an emergency alarm rang out. A Scarer named George had returned from the human world with a child's sock on his back!

In seconds, a squad from the CDA (Child Detection Agency) arrived to decontaminate him.

When work was finished, Mike rushed to meet his girlfriend, Celia. They had planned a special date.

But Roz, the company's cranky file clerk, blocked Mike's way. Mike had forgotten to file his Scare reports! Sulley kindly offered to help.

BOO!

Back on the Scare Floor, Sulley noticed that someone had left a door behind. Sulley peeked through the door. "Hello? Is anybody scaring in here?" he called out. As the Scarer turned to leave, he heard a thump. Then he felt something tug on his tail. Sulley turned around. There was a little girl clinging to his tail!

"Kitty!" the girl called to the big, furry monster.

Meanwhile, Mike and Celia were enjoying a romantic dinner. Mike was telling Celia what a beautiful monster she was when he looked up and saw Sulley waving frantically outside the restaurant window. He looked terrified!

Sulley came inside and told Mike about the child. Mike was horrified . . . especially when Sulley showed him the little girl. He had brought her with him!

The little girl wiggled away from Sulley and began running around the restaurant, scaring the monsters. When the CDA arrived, Mike and Sulley hid the child in a take-out box and ran. They were in big trouble!

Back in their apartment, Sulley and Mike tried not to touch the child. Mike even put on oven mitts and flippers to protect himself!

Then Mike accidentally fell down. The little girl started to giggle. As she laughed, the lights burned brighter and brighter. Suddenly—*pop!*—they burned out completely.

Finally, Sulley put the child to bed. But she was afraid.

Sulley realized she was scared that Randall was in the closet. He must be her Scarer! Sulley showed her that there were no monsters in the closet and then stayed with her until she fell asleep.

"This might sound crazy," Sulley told Mike, "but I don't think that kid is dangerous."

The next day, Sulley and Mike disguised the girl as a monster and returned to Monsters, Inc. They hoped to find her door and send her home before anyone found out she was there. But when they arrived, the company was crawling with CDA agents. Luckily, the disguise fooled everyone. Sulley and Mike quickly walked past the agents.

In the locker room, Sulley and the child played hide-and-seek. "Boo!" she said playfully.

Sulley smiled back at her. He was really starting to like her!

Just then they overheard Randall tell his assistant that he planned to take care of the kid.

Sulley needed to get the child home before Randall could do something bad to her.

Mike snuck out of the bathroom and arranged to have the child's door brought to the Scare Floor. But he made a mistake.

"This isn't Boo's door," Sulley exclaimed.

"Boo!?!" Mike couldn't believe Sulley had named the kid.

Suddenly the other Scarers and the CDA agents appeared on the Scare Floor.

Randall's Secret

Sulley moved to hide Boo, but she was gone!

Mike and Sulley split up to find her, but Randall cornered Mike. The monster knew all about Boo. He ordered Mike to bring her back to the Scare Floor. He said he'd have her door ready.

Sulley found Boo, and together they found Mike. Mike told his friend about Randall's plan to send Boo home. Together they went to the Scare Floor. The door was waiting for them, but Sulley was worried. "We can't trust Randall," he said.

Mike disagreed. To prove the door was safe, he went through—and was captured by Randall!

Sulley and Boo secretly followed Randall. They learned that he had invented a new way to capture screams. And he was about to try it on Mike!

Sulley rescued Mike, and the friends ran toward the training room. They had to warn their boss, Mr. Waternoose.

Sulley and Mike told Mr. Waternoose everything. But before they could do anything else to save Boo, she accidentally saw Sulley looking scary. He tried to calm her down, but she was terrified of him.

Sulley felt awful. For the first time, he realized how mean it was to scare a child.

Mr. Waternoose promised to fix everything, but he was really working with Randall! The CEO of Monsters, Inc. shoved Sulley and Mike through a door into the human world. They were banished to the Himalayan Mountains! Even worse, Mr. Waternoose and Randall had Boo!

Sulley knew that Boo was in trouble. He raced to the nearest village and found a closet that would lead him home. Then he rushed to Randall's secret lab.

Boo was strapped to Randall's machine. Sulley roared and tore the machine apart.

As Sulley raced away with Boo, Mike arrived to help. But Celia couldn't understand what was going on. Mike quickly explained about Boo and about Randall's evil plan. Celia didn't believe Mike. But when she saw Randall chasing after him, she realized Mike was telling the truth.

Mike and Sulley climbed onto the machine
that carried doors to the Scare Floor. They had to
get Boo home! But the power wasn't on.
Mike made a funny face and Boo laughed.
The power surged, and the doors began to move.

Mike and Sulley still had a problem. They couldn't put Boo through just *any* door. They had to find *her* door!

The trio jumped in and out of closets, until at last, Randall grabbed Boo. But Boo fought back!

"She's not scared of you anymore," Sulley told Randall.

Working together, Boo, Mike, and Sulley beat Randall once and for all.

But Sulley, Mike, and Boo weren't safe yet. Mr. Waternoose and the CDA were controlling the doors. While Mike distracted the agents, Sulley escaped with Boo. Unfortunately, Mr. Waternoose saw everything. "Give me the child," he yelled, running after Sulley.

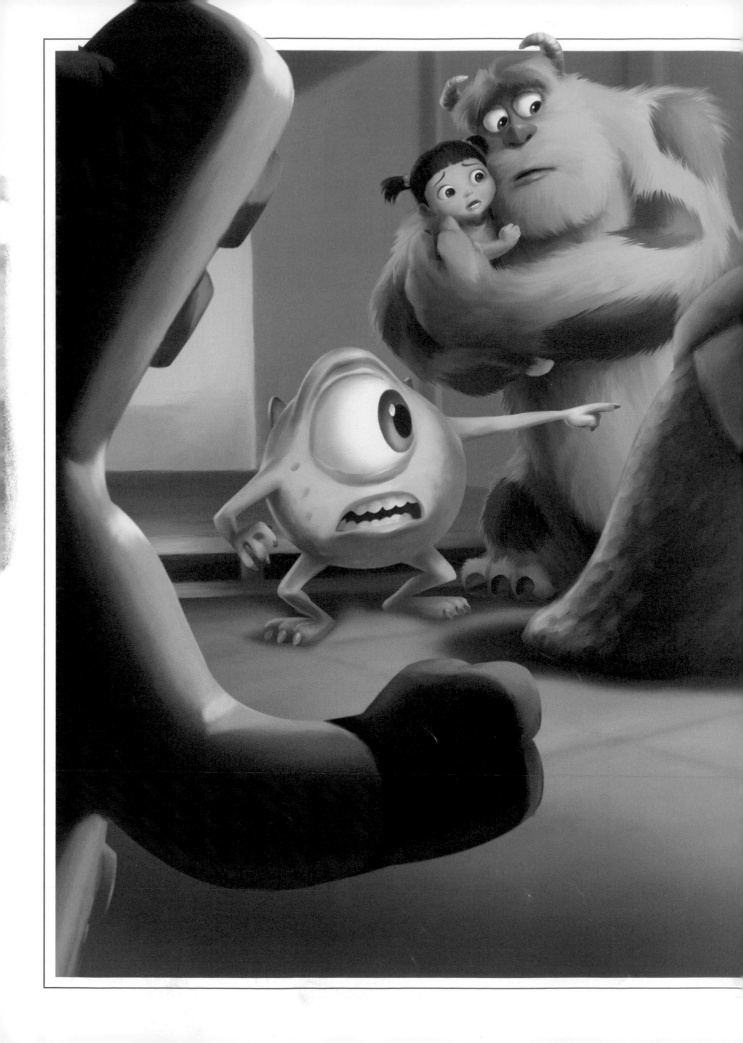

While Mr. Waternoose raced after Sulley, Mike recorded him saying, "I'll kidnap a thousand children before I let this company die!"

Mike broadcast his words to everyone. Now all of Monstropolis knew that Mr. Waternoose planned to take children. He was arrested by the head of the CDA—Roz!

It was time for Boo to go home. Sulley followed her into her room. Gently, he tucked her into bed. Sulley sadly returned to Monstropolis. Roz ordered the CDA to shred Boo's door. It wouldn't be used for scaring anymore.

After that, Sulley became president of Monsters, Inc. And the Scare Floor became a Laugh Floor! It was all because Sulley had discovered that laughter produced more power than screams.

Monsters, Inc. and Monstropolis were saved!

Sulley still missed Boo, though. He had one tiny sliver of her door, but the rest had been destroyed.

One day, Mike surprised his pal. He'd put the door back together! It was missing just one little piece. Sulley inserted the piece, opened the door, and saw . . .

"Boo?" Sulley whispered.
"Kitty!" an excited voice replied.
The two friends were reunited at last.